See Pip Point

For Carole and Zane

Atheneum Books for Young Readers
An imprint of Simon & Schuster Children's Publishing Division
1230 Avenue of the Americas
New York, New York 10020

Book design by Sonia Chaghatzbanian
The text for this book is set in Century Oldstyle.
The illustrations for this book are rendered in digital pen-and-ink.

Printed in the United States of America
First Edition

2 4 6 8 10 9 7 5 3 1

Library of Congress Cataloging-in-Publication Data
Milgrim, David.
See Pip point / David Milgrim.—1st ed.
p.   cm.
Summary: When Pip the mouse floats off with Otto the robot's
balloon, Otto and Zee the Bee go to the rescue.
ISBN 0-689-85116-2
[1. Mice—Fiction. 2. Robots—Fiction. 3. Bees—Fiction.
4. Friendship—Fiction. 5. Balloons—Fiction.] I. Title.
PZ7 .M5995 Se 2003
[E]—dc21   2002005289

See Pip Point

story and pictures by
D AV I D   M I LG R I M

Atheneum Books for Young Readers
New York London Toronto Sydney Singapore

See Pip.
See Pip point.

Point, point, point.
Point, point, point.
Point, point, point.

See Otto share.

Thank you,
Otto.

Oops,
there goes Pip.

See Pip go.

Go, go, go.

Uh-oh.

See Pip go up.
See Pip go way up.
See Pip go up, up,
and away.

See Zee the Bee.
See Zee the Bee fly.
See Zee the Bee fly
in his sleep.

See Pip go down.
See Pip go way down.
See Pip go down,
down to the ground.

Look! Here comes Otto!
Hurry, Otto, hurry!

See Otto save Pip!
Thank you, Otto!

Uh-oh.

See Otto and Pip crash.

See Otto and Pip splash.

Oops.

See Pip point.